WILL

and the

Garden of Life

Brother David

Brother David

© **2021**

DEDICATION

This book is dedicated to

All those who put

Galatians 5.22-23

Into practice.

****

TABLE OF CONTENTS

1 Seeing the land---Building the wall

2 Who cleared the land, Will?

3 Those are names?

4 Who is knocking?

5 Opening the door to freedom

6 Clearing the way for perfection

7 The attack from without

   My it's getting cold in here

8 A rescue attack

9 The fruit of change

10 Total destruction

11 Total renewal

12 The village under the bridge

13 Pastor Johnson

14 The garden of chains

15	Come on home Mom
16	A new home for the homeless
17	Ground hogs under the garden
18	Constructing more than a building
19	The farmers market
20	The Mayor
21	Down in the dumps but not for long

1

SEEING THE LAND--
BUILDING THE WALL

There was a very special young man who one day received a very unique present. This very special present was a piece of land. Although that may sound strange to you, the young man was thrilled with this special gift.

As he stood at the front edge of his land that first morning, he started thinking about what he wanted to do with it, this "Garden of Life," as he called it.

The first thing he wanted to do was to build a large, stone wall around it and then put in place a strong wooden gate with a large wooden bar to hold the gate closed. Then he thought,

"After I have built the wall and gate, I will build a little house for myself. After that, I will clear the land of everything and plant beautiful flowers, bushes, vines, vegetables and trees."

With the energy of a hundred men, he set about building the very strong stone wall around the entire property. Day after day, from the first peaks of light to the last rays of the sun, this young man, whom I will call Will, worked and worked. Never once did he let up. Never once was he discouraged or defeated at the amount of work he had to do. Day after day he built on, until one day he saw the place where he had begun the wall coming into view.

"The end is near," he thought. "The end is very near."

At the close of the next day he put the final rock into place and hung the giant wooden gate in the gap he had left for it. The final act was to put into place the strong timber that would bar the gate so no intruders could come in.

With a good night's sleep, he then tackled building his own little house. That, too, he finished quickly. With the house finished, Will thought to himself,

"Tomorrow I can start clearing the land and begin planting the seeds and plants that will transform this weed-filled land into my Garden of Life."

With so much done, Will actually slept in. When he finally got up it was well into the morning hours. As he stepped out on his front porch, he was already thinking to himself about where he was going to start clearing his garden and what the first things that he was going to plant would be.

2

WHO CLEARED THE LAND, WILL?

As his eyes began to focus on his land, he was shocked beyond belief. His garden had been cleared of all the weeds he didn't want and new plants and trees had been planted all over it. These new things were growing like wildfire right before his eyes! Trees were growing up into the sky as he watched. Vines were curling their way everywhere. The bushes were already ripe with new fruit. This, he thought, was impossible. How could the land have been cleared and then replanted overnight? And how could the things that were planted be growing so fast and be bearing fruit so quickly? It was way more than his mind could comprehend.

Then he began to hear some noise coming from the back of the garden. Leaving his porch on a dead run, he headed in the direction of the noise. As he got to where the noise was coming from, he saw a figure of what appeared to be a man clearing the land and planting new seeds and roots. These new seeds and roots were sprouting and growing quickly, even before he could take a step. Tapping The Stranger on the shoulder, Will said in as loud of a voice as he could,

"I'm Will and who are you and how did you get into my Garden of Life?"

Without even responding to Will's questions, The Stranger turned around and began to speak to Will in a strange kind of way. His speech was rapid, convincing, and controlling. He didn't allow Will to get a word in edgewise. He 'ran the show,' as some would say. The Stranger controlled Will from that moment on.

"Well, Will, I was waiting for you. I knew that you would hear me in the back of the garden and would find your way here. I also knew that you were very, very tired from all the work that you have put in, so I decided to give you a hand by clearing and planting this garden for you."

Because The Stranger's speech was rapid and so controlling, Will was left at a loss to know what to do or say.

"Here, Will," said The Stranger. "Some of the new fruit is already ripe. Try it! I know that you will like it and will really come to enjoy it."

Even before Will could make up his mind whether or take some or not, The Stranger had picked a piece of fruit and was almost forcing it into Will's mouth. Before Will knew it, he was eating it.

"Well, the taste isn't that bad," said Will, so he kept on eating it. Suddenly, he got a sharp, stabbing pain that caused him to bend over from the cramps that were in his stomach. But even in that great pain, Will kept on trying the samples of fruit that were being forced upon him. Even though they were sweet in his mouth, the more he ate, the more the pain in his stomach got worse.

As Will walked around the garden, listening to The Stranger, he couldn't stop sampling the fruit. With each bite he got sicker. This went on day after day after day. Will got sicker and sicker and The Stranger kept clearing and planting. Will couldn't help himself and so kept eating, although he was getting weaker and sicker all the time. The Stranger had gotten control of Will by now and was doing whatever he wanted to do in Will's Garden of Life.

Several days later Will finally got away from The Stranger and headed for the far side of the garden. As he walked next to the little stream that flowed through the center of it, he looked down into the water and saw a reflection of his face. To his horror, he looked almost like a beast, a wild animal. His hair was long and matted. His skin looked like a dry piece of leather. His eyes appeared to be narrow and angry. He had changed so much he could hardly believe that such a change was possible.

Will became so angry that he ran to his house and found an axe that he had on the front porch. With the axe in hand, he began chopping at the fruit in the garden, cutting it down to the ground. He was swinging away at the plants like a mad man. His only desire was to get rid of the fruit. Even though he was so weak from eating it, he did not let up. However, as he looked back over his shoulder at what he had cut down, he saw, to his horror, that the fruit had begun to re-grow and was in full bloom again. Will did not realize that he was not able to kill the plants because he had not killed the roots, which were deep in the ground.

3

THOSE ARE NAMES

Will's anger then boiled over. Running through the garden, he found The Stranger bent over, working. Whirling him around, Will said to him,

"I've tried day after day to get the names of these fruits out of you, but you have avoided me. Now, right now, not in a few minutes, I want the names of these fruits that I keep eating and eating."

For several seconds The Stranger didn't answer Will. Then, in a very soft and almost inaudible voice, he began to list the names of the fruits that he had planted in the Garden of Life—

"Anger, hate, fighting, swearing, disobedience to parents, killing, stealing, cheating."

Just hearing these awful names made Will put his hands over his ears so that he didn't have to hear any more names. He walked over to a tree and sat down on the ground. Putting his back against the tree, he put his head in his hands and began to sob uncontrollably. He was now totally controlled by The Stranger. He couldn't stop eating and eating the fruit. Even while he sat there sobbing, he reached out and ate more fruit and got sick all over again. For most of the day he sat there and cried. The Stranger went to some other part of the garden, laughing all the way with a sick, sneering laugh.

4

WHO IS KOCKING?

As Will sat there with his head in his hands, he started to hear a tiny whisper. It was very soft and hardly audible. Yet, he never raised his head to see where it was coming from.

"Will, behold I stand at the door and knock. Please let me in, Will, please let me in."

This whisper went on for several minutes, but Will never raised his head. Then the whisper got a little louder.

"Behold I stand at the door and knock. Please let me in, Will, please let me in."

Still Will didn't raise his head. He didn't realize there was a figure at the front gate of his Garden of Life. The figure at the gate raised his voice a third time and said,

"Will, please let me in. I am standing at your garden's gate. Please let me in."

Without raising his head, Will said in a strong, loud voice,

"Look, whoever you are, I am not going to let anyone else into this garden, my Garden of Life. I don't know who you are and I am not going to find out. Go away! Leave me alone! I have been tricked once. I am not going to be tricked again and have things turn even worse than what they are now. **GO—A—WAY!!**

In the back of the garden The Stranger heard the voices. He knew who was at the front gate and took off running through the garden, yelling,

"Don't let him in, Will, don't let him in. If you do, he will ruin everything."

When he reached the front he saw what appeared to be a young Prince at the gate who apparently had come from a recent battle. There were fresh scars on his head and hands.

The Stranger began to yell louder and louder into Wills ear,

"Don't let him in, Will, don't let him in. If you do, Will, he will ruin everything that I have done. He will destroy everything, and I mean everything.

5

OPENING THE DOOR TO FREEDOM

When Will heard that **everything** in the garden would be ruined, he jumped up from his seat under the tree and gave the giant bar on the front gate a big kick. As the bar went flying, the gate opened and allowed the young Prince to walk in. Will was excited to see what the reaction was going to be on The Stranger's face. But as he turned around, The Stranger wasn't there. He had disappeared.

"If The Stranger said the truth," Will said to the Prince, "then destroy this garden of fruit and destroy it right now."

The young Prince motioned to Will and they began to walk together down through the garden. Just one look from the Prince and the fruit began to die **from the root up.** As they walked and walked, things were dying as fast as they had grown. Will began to feel more and more excited. Soon the garden would be empty of all that The Stranger had planted, and he would be able to plant what he wanted.

As they came to the back of the garden, Will turned around and looked back over the garden. To his amazement and shock, new fruit was growing right where the old fruit had died. New and different fruit was growing up quickly in the same way the old fruit had grown.

"You tricked me," Will yelled, "I don't know how you did it, but you tricked me. You have planted the garden all over again with your own fruit. You tricked me, you tricked me, you tricked me!"

Will was frustrated and furious. The young Prince said in a strong and quiet voice,

"Before you pass judgment, Will, I want you to try some of the fruit."

"Sure, sure," said Will. "More fruit and more stabbing pain, more stomach aches."

With some reluctance, Will took a sample from the young Prince and bit in. It wasn't too bad. The taste in his mouth was a gentle sweetness. A few second later, as Will kept eating, his stomach began to feel a lot better. The more he ate, the better he felt. Soon he felt absolutely wonderful.

'"What are the names of these fruits you have planted in my Garden of Life?" Will asked.

"Well," said the Prince, "there are only nine kinds of fruit here in your Garden of Life. They **are LOVE, JOY, PEACE, LONG-SUFFERING, GENTLENESS, GOODNESS, FAITH, MEEKNESS and SELF-CONTROL.** These are the names of the fruits that I have planted in your Garden of Life."

Over the next several days all of The Stranger's fruit was killed with just one look from the young Prince. As the young Prince and Will walked through the garden, they passed by the stream where Will had once seen his hideous reflection. This time he saw a kind and gentle face which filled him with joy.

With each passing day, Will felt new strength as he ate fruit that the young Prince had planted. A new gentleness came to his mind and a peace that he had never known filled his heart. The young Prince assured Will that although The Stranger was gone for a moment, he would attempt one day to get back into the garden.

"But remember, Will, I will never leave you. I will always be here to protect you and your Garden of Life."

6

CLEARING THE WAY FOR PERFECTION

The days that followed the ouster of The Stranger were wonderful days, days beyond belief. The Young Prince worked tirelessly on Will's behalf, helping him reclaim his Garden of Life from the damage The Stranger had inflicted.

It was no easy task, for the work of The Stranger had been extensive. 'Rooting out' the damage was quite time consuming because of the vast size of his Garden of Life.

Each day Will tried to concentrate on eating one of the nine fruits that the Young Prince had planted. Each one was unique, different, and oh yes, unusual. Each one seemed to do something different in him, to him, or, I could say, on him.

It seemed that each fruit addressed different feelings and thoughts that he had in him. Not everything in him was 'wonderful or marvelous', as the song says. Many things in him you would never see or even know about, but as he would take a piece of a particular fruit it seemed to be like a tool of the Young Prince in him. As it only took one look from the Prince to kill the fruit of The Stranger from the root up, so to it seemed that each fruit shone a light upon things in him that needed to die from the 'root up.'

All of this was not easy. Pulling roots up out of dirt is a whole lot easier than things that are in your life being torn away so that they don't grow to a point that they are controlling you.

You can't imagine nine different, totally different tastes to try. This fruit of the Prince is so tasty and filling and even wonderful to smell. The fragrance that would go into the air from just one bite was beyond his skill to describe.

Not only did Will have nine delicacies of the Prince to indulge in continuously throughout the day, but he had the thrill of interacting with this warrior, The Young Prince.

Will found it hard to comprehend that all he cared about was his' Garden of Life.' He failed to focus on anything but his Garden.

7

THE ATTACK FROM WITHOUT

MY IT'S GETTING COLD IN HERE

Each day Will lived from morning to night focusing on his Garden and all of the details of having such a place.

He failed to notice that each day there was less and less sunlight shining on his garden. The morning light came later and later and the afternoon light left earlier and earlier. Although the sun hadn't set, it just seemed that in fact the sun had set, if you know what I mean.

Will failed to ask himself why these things were happening. THAT WAS WRONG. He failed also to give any thought to where The Stranger had gone when the Young Prince came in. I guess he assumed he just went away, never to be heard from again. THAT WAS WRONG. That was a fatal mistake.

As there started to be less and less sunlight, it started to have an impact on the growth and health of the things in the Garden. The plants in his Garden thrived on sun and warmth and a lot of water. But suddenly all of that was being diminished. There was less sun, which meant less warmth in the air and there was much less water to keep the plants lively. The cool weather started changing the appearance of all the plants. They just started looking sick.

Then one day Will looked 'up,' all around the perimeter of his large Garden. It was then he noticed an incredible sight. All around the perimeter large trees were growing up at an astounding rate. Not only were they growing each and every day by leaps and bounds, but they were closely packed together with intertwining foliage. This was creating a wall in the sky. Although the sun came up, its effects could not be felt until it was basically overhead. Its warmth and light were blocked out until midday and then were gone by early afternoon.

When Will began to realize what was happening he sounded the alarm to the Prince. The Prince asked Will an all important question,

"Where do you think these trees came from? Who planted them? Who would try to hurt you and your Garden of Life?"

The answer, because the questions had been asked so well, was obvious,The Stranger. He was still at work trying to destroy what the Prince had done and in the process destroying Will's life and this gift that had been given to him.

As Will talked with the Prince and started figuring out what was going on, he was left with important questions: How to destroy the Stranger's work? How to get rid of this wall of trees? How to restore sunlight his Garden?

8

A RESCUE ATTACK

Will knew that even if he left his Garden and tried to cut down the trees, it would become clear very quickly that it would be an impossible human task. Divine intervention was going to be necessary for these trees and their foliage to be done away with.

Although the Prince sure was extra ordinary and maybe even divine, Will didn't know if he could get rid of so much that was growing taller, stronger and more dense every hour. He could see his Garden becoming an ice skating rink if something didn't happen soon.

The Young Prince challenged Will to think what a challenge in itself was. He asked him,

"Have you ever walked through your Garden and just touched different plants, just saying, 'Thank you?' Even though I might have put the seeds in the ground you need to ask yourself, "Who gave me those seeds? Who told me to come here to the Garden? Who told me to do what in the Garden of Life?"

"I think you should consider doing that. You need to express yourself out loud. You need to be appreciative of this gift, this Garden of Life, and the fruit that you are enjoying.

"Next, I think you are right. I think that you need to sit down in the center of the Garden and call for divine intervention. You need to call on God to strip the foliage from those trees and allow the supernatural light from the sun in once again, as it was in the beginning. Young one, Will, the lack of light is going to kill this Garden. You need the supernatural qualities of the sun to be unleashed again upon your place here.

"But it's going start with the fertilizer of gratefulness from you. Divine intervention will come if your heart is genuine about this problem. When the two meet, victory over this problem will quickly come also."

Will sure had received 'divine instruction' to go with divine intervention. Sitting in the middle of his Garden of Life caused him to cry out on behalf of this gift that had been given to him. Everything about what he had was unique and special. It was like nothing else he had ever seen. It was dying and it broke his heart. He didn't want The Stranger's acts to win and destroy what the Prince had done and his gift, this Garden, this Garden he called Life.

Will really don't know how long he cried out, but certainly it was hours, not minutes. Then he started walking through the Garden, touching everything and speaking out loud words of thanks. For hours he walked and walked through the Garden. His voice became louder and louder as he expressed his gratefulness. The more he spoke the louder he became. He felt so empowered. As he got to the end of his 'bless'n time' he was so excited about what he was doing that he was shouting.

As Will was completing his walk through the Garden, he heard a horrible sound in the air. A deafening sound. A frightful sound. He dove for the protection of his little house.

The air suddenly became black with flying insects. These insects shut out the sun's light completely. They filled every square inch of every tree The Stranger had planted, and feasted on the leaves and foliage. Their 'stripping' sound caused Will to put his hands over his ears. It was loud and yes, quite scary, it was so unusual.

Minute after minute they feasted on the green leaves and tender bark. Feasting on the bark killed the life of the trees.

Then this black cloud filled the air and hovered there, making a hideous, downright scary sound. He was sure this sound could be heard for miles and miles, since it was so loud, and this infestation of bugs covered such a large portion of the sky.

Then suddenly, with dramatic speed, they were gone. The trees were stripped and dead, and the power and work of the sun was restored.

Will's Garden seemed to almost exhale and began to rebound and grow again. It was quickly being restored to its former beauty and grandeur. As the vitality of the plants began to rapidly be restored, Will started enjoying and "thanking" for each mouthful he ate.

Although the Garden was grand, the death outside the wall was truly sickening. Trees by the hundreds stood dead and lifeless. There was forever, it seemed, a message to Will from the dead trees. It was so sad to see them standing there, without life, but they had been so dangerous for the life of his Garden.

But on a positive note, The Strangers work had been killed.

Was he dead? OH NO, NO, NO. The enemy to Will's Garden of Life is out there somewhere plotting his next attack and Will needed to learn from the Prince how to properly stand against this Stranger whose goal for him and this Garden was death. The attack marks left upon the Young Prince for doing so were quite visible and unbelievably deep, with death also being the goal.

I needed to learn a great deal more from the Young Prince. I can't get myself needlessly into another bad event like this one. Oh that the Wisdom that I need might fall upon me so living would be victorious.

9

THE FRUIT OF CHANGE

Even though it was very early in the morning, Will was up and at'em. One thing that struck him was the fact that his Garden had enough fruit in it to easily feed 'a hundred people,' as he put it. So Will got an idea, and in short order built it: a fruit cart. In no time at all Will had loaded the cart with about eight or ten items of each of the nine fruits.

Will was so amazed that his cart pushed like a feather with so many things on it. As he started down High Street he saw a boy about ten years old bouncing a basket ball in the drive way of his home. Will yelled out to him,

"Hey, young man, I've got some free fruit to give away. Come and get as much as you want."

Without a moment's hesitation the boy, whose name was Chuck, came running over to Will's cart and took one each from about four kinds. Soon he was yelling at Will, as Will headed down the street on a very sunny day,

"Love it man. Love it!"

Will started to make his way down the street and in the next block passed a group of girls playing Hop-Scotch on the sidewalk. Soon they, too, were eating up the fruit from Will's Garden of Life.

As Will started pushing his cart away, all six girls came running after him, begging for 'seconds' and 'thirds.' Will didn't hesitate to give the girls his fruit. He even gave each one a couple of pieces of fruit to take to her parents.

When Will came to the corner of the highway and High Street, he just sat there, giving fruit away to all who passed by. People couldn't believe that someone was giving away such beautiful fruit for free. Then, when the effects of the fruit set in, they raved loudly about the fruit. With the fruit being so beautiful to look at, so rich in taste and so filling, Will was beginning to have a following. All afternoon people kept coming to Will's fruit cart as they heard about it from their friends.

Then a phenomenal thing began to happen. People started coming back to the cart wanting to know all about the fruit itself. They started telling Will about the changes that had come over them because of the fruit they had eaten.

The trip home that afternoon was like a parade. People were coming from everywhere, seeking a piece of fruit to eat. Fruit that they were saying was sooo good in their mouth and unbelievable in their stomach. Yet many were saying that there was some kind of transformative powers to the fruit. One unusual thing was the fact that on the way home, Will had just as much fruit on the cart as he had when he started out that morning. No one missed out getting fruit if they came to Will. Talk about an instant success!! Will was so excited about his fruit cart experience he couldn't stop talking it to the Prince when he got back to his Garden of Life.

Early the next morning he could hear a child's voice calling. out. Quickly he came to the front gate and saw the boy from across the street standing there, beating on the gate and yelling for him. Even before the gate was completely opened Charlie was begging to Will to

"Follow me, Mister. Hurry up sir, and follow me."

And with that, Charlie was on the move. Will actually had to start jogging to catch up with him.

As they got to the young boy's house across the street the boy started shouting at Will,

"Look man, look at all that stuff that's growing in my yard. Look!! Look!! I took the seeds from the fruit you gave me yesterday and put them in the dirt over there and well, look at all that stuff. It's huge. It's unbelievable how fast it's growing. At this rate I'll even have some fruit tomorrow, I bet."

Sure enough, Charlie had three, four and some five foot high vines, bushes and fruit trees growing. And it was probably true, he would have fruit in a day or two. Not just some fruit, but a whole lot of fruit.

"Man," said Charlie, "I'm look'n right at an unbelievable miracle. I am look'n at a miracle! No one is going to believe me no matter what I say. No one."

Charlie was probably right, fruit trees in a day!
P H E N O M E N A L!!!

"And of all things, Mister Will, what in the world has happened to me, my Mom wants to know? She said that my nasty mouth has totally disappeared. She said I have started obeying her like I was an obedient angel. Everything she ask me to do I tell her, 'Yes Ma'am'. She thinks I've had a brain transplant or some'n like that."

Will exploded into laughter that could be heard a block away. All Will did was wave at Charlie and head home to The Garden. He had a cart to fill up.

10

TOTAL DISTRUCTION TOTAL RENEWAL

Because of the things that happened yesterday, Will couldn't wait to get going with his cart today. So with a VERY full cart, he was off, heading south on Hickory Point Drive.

It was a couple of blocks of walking before Will bumped into anyone. Right on the corner of Hickory Point and Elm Street was a house and garden that was really hurting and I mean hurting bad. The house was run down in every way. There wasn't a thing that it didn't need. Things were broken, dirty, unpainted, way out of date, and in need of repair. The destruction of the wall around the property was almost beyond belief. Stones were loose, gone, and piled on the ground. The gate was a disaster. Whatever was left of it was worthless.

As Will stood there in the street looking at the major disaster, John, the owner, for no reason at all came running out of his garden. He started yelling and complaining to Will. The volume of his rant was off the volume charts. He had no coherence about his rant. It was about this and it was about that. It was his fault or their fault.

"Oh no, not me," he screamed. He went on and on and on without making any sense, any sense at all.

As John was screaming at Will, Will simply grabbed a peachy colored fruit and put it to the man's mouth. Before he even knew what had happened, John was gobbling up the fruit like there was no tomorrow. When he had finished it, even without asking, he ate another and then another and yes a fourth. Then he stood there in a state of total and complete calm. Peace had dropped in on him like a cloud burst. He just stood there baffled, as Will was, about the change that had come over him.

The Young Prince, who had been following Will from a distance just to see what Will was experiencing, walked over to the man's garden and just stood and stared at all the mess. The garden was totally overgrown. No one with a hundred men could have cleared it. Weeds were densely intertwined, thick with vines and overgrowth, and filled with all sorts of terrible creatures. As the Prince stood there, staring intently at the mountain of mess, all of a sudden the material in the garden began to evaporate. It was dissolving right before Will's and John's eyes. Animals of all types started making a great escape. The power of the Prince's look terrified anything that was alive in the weeds. There started a new kind of migration down the street, right before our eyes.

In no time at all 'Mr. Calm and Quiet John' was on his knees next to the Prince, weeping for joy at the ongoing miracle.

Finally every, weed, twig, branch, vine, and wild tree was gone. The sight of a garden of just dirt and more dirt left everyone who was watching it all just speechless.

Quickly the seeds from John's fruit were in the ground. No one knows how it happened, but the next morning every stone of John's garden wall was cemented in place and a new wooden gate was installed with a beautiful bar across the inside.

11

MEETING THE WILD MAN

As Will went down the street, he kept tossing different kind's fruit people's way. Sometime later that morning he came upon the most famous man in the area. He was famous to everyone because he was the 'wild man of the valley.' He was unbelievably insane. He never hurt anyone but he was everywhere screaming at the sun, at the moon, at the clouds and at anything that came his way. He terrified children because he had a long beard and an inadequate amount of clothing. He would sit on the curb of the road and cry for hours. No one knew of anything that had helped him or could help him.

As Will got close to 'Wild', as he was called, he took one piece of each of the nine fruits and carried them over to Wild. Even before Will could give them all to him,

Wild, like the wild man he was, was eating them. Somewhere during the eating of the fourth or fifth piece of fruit, a veil of calm started to fall upon Wild. You could see it fall so gently and so powerfully. Even Wild's eyes started to show a quietness and a lack of fear. As Wild sat there he started to cry out loud,

"Dear God help me. Bring me back from Hell."

He ate piece seven and then piece eight and then began to cry for joy as he started into the peachy ninth piece. Wild consumed that piece in but a moment. Then he cried out in a pitiful way,

"Will anyone here help me? I want to be set free. Help me someone. Help me, please."

Will filled he arms with three of the fruits and went over and sat down next to Wild. Soon these fruits were gone and the scars and mars all over the man's body began to disappear. He said,

"Sir, my name isn't Wild anymore. I think I should be called Mr. Peace. Yes, Sir, I would like to be called Mr. Peace from now on."

Whatever change had come over Peace in those few minutes was nothing like what he was like in the days that followed. For many weeks he and Will were inseparable. Every day that Will went down the street with his fruit cart, Peace was quietly at his side. With his hair and beard cut and new clothes on, many didn't know him as the man they had called Wild. In fact the legend of Wild slowly disappeared and the stories about a 'peace worker in town' started to grow.

Soon you could see in the far north regions of our area, a man with a cart full of fruit walking along, giving special gifts to the hopeless and needy, the downcast and even the sick. No one connected the fact that the man with this cart was the wild man from two weeks ago. He spoke so softly that people had to stand very quietly to hear him. His gentleness with children left adults speechless.

Then one day Amy Snyder said to Peace,

"Aren't you the veterinarian that used to have a clinic on the east side of town about fifteen years ago?"

For a few seconds Peace just stood there with his head hung low, then he said to Amy,

"Yes, that was me. I did some things that really destroyed my family, my medical practice, and most of all my life. It made me go literally insane. If it hadn't been for my friend Will who wasn't afraid of me, I would still be insane and homeless. I am just hoping that I don't scare anyone now. My life, I pray, is a life of peace and love to all I meet."

"Do you know where any members of your family are right now, Peace?" Amy asked.

"No I don't. I wouldn't even know how to find any of them. I'm sure they are all alive, though, including my wife."

Amy sat down with Peace and told him that she was a genealogist. She told Peace that if he would let her, she would like to help him find all of his family, including his parents, who might be still living. With just a simple nod of his head, Amy began writing down the answers to her questions that she asked Peace. As she asked questions Peace gave her two light green pieces of fruit to eat. She finished them and said with a grin on her face,

"More. Give me more, man." Then she and Peace laughed and laughed.

Each day as she was out jogging Amy would let Peace know that she hadn't forgotten him and that she and her staff were working on finding all his relatives.

After only a week and a half, Amy was joined by two members of her staff in the park by the Garden. There she sat down with Peace and she even invited Will, whom she had learned about over the last couple of weeks.

"Peace, do you know what your real name is?" Amy asked.

For a few seconds Peace just sat there and didn't respond. Then he said,

"Yes, I know that my name is Dr. Mark Harris. I know that I was a well known vet in this town. The name Peace better suits me now, I think. I made a mess of that name and I am quite ashamed of it. Yet, I must say, Will has made sure that it isn't his fruit but who he is that loves me. Thank God for Will and his genuine heart."

"Well, Peace," said Amy. "Finding some of the things about you was, well, quite easy. Would you look at the girl on the end of the table for me? Do you recognize her?"

As Amy said that, the girl on the end had a surge of tears flowing down her face.

"Peace, Kelly Peterson is a member of my staff and she is your youngest daughter."

In a blink, Peace and his daughter were sobbing in each other's arms. After a few minutes Amy had Peace and his daughter sit down together. Amy turned to Kelly and said to her,

"Why don't you tell your dad the rest of the story?" Kelly cleared her throat and turned to her dad.

"All of us are still alive, dad. All of us have gone to college and are married except for me. But my wedding is only five weeks away. You have four grand children, two each from Bud and Kathy. Both live about one hour away from the city. As for Mom, she…," Kelly's voice broke as she said, "As for Mom, she's walking up right behind you right now!"

Whirling around, Peace saw someone coming up the hill behind him, openly crying. Without a moment's hesitation, Peace ran into the open arms of the lady, his wife. How glad everyone was that Amy brought several boxes of tissue.

Then it became altogether too much for Peace. He was so overwhelmed with emotion that he sank to the ground and wailed. Valery, his wife, sank down next to him and softly talked to him. For all of us, this was just an emotionally staggering moment.

Finally some of Will's ice cold water and some blushing red fruit brought peace to the man called Peace.

Then across the park came two men, two women and four young children. Yes, it was Peace's boys with their wives and his four grand children. Thankfully the two boys reached out to their dad with honest and sincere love. Because Mark had changed so much over the years as he became Wild, the two boys didn't recognize him when they would pass him on the city streets and really didn't care about finding him because of all the things he had done. But with Amy and her staff's help, they had come to see if it was worth meeting their dad again.

It would take some time and planning before Peace and his wife would restore their marriage.

Then one evening Kelly and her fiancé stopped in to see Mark.

"Dad," Kelly said, "I've talked with Mom and Jim, and we're all in agreement. Would you walk me down the aisle when I get married in two weeks?"

Peace was speechless. Softly he said to Kelly,

"I would be so honored. Thank you and Jim so much. Wow, what a thrill awaits me, Kelly. What a thrill awaits me!"

12

THE VILLAGE UNDER THE BRIDGE

One of the unique features about Will's garden was the extremely cold spring water in the stream that ran through it. It was so cold that you would think that it was more ice than water.

One day Will got an idea. Many places close to his garden had construction taking place. Summertime is a very tough time for outdoor construction workers to stay cool and hydrated. Will got the idea to get some containers, put them in a big box and pack the box with insulation. Then he would fill the containers with his icy cold water and see if that could be of some help to the workers as they worked under the blazing sun.

In addition to his fruit, Will now was becoming known as the 'ice-man.' His ice cold water was a welcomed blessing to all the outdoor workers, in addition to the fruit he distributed regularly.

There was an area in the city that was never talked about, but was such a big eye sore. Underneath one of the city's main bridges was an area that had been taken over by the homeless. They lived there in makeshift tents and boxes. No one talked about it, and no one did anything to change it. Out of sight, out of mind was the way that most people looked at it. They were all sorts of people living under the bridge. Living under the bridge meant that they were difficult to see, if at all.

With his cart stacked high with his beautiful and delicious fruit, Will determined to go to that area to see if his fruit could change minds and heart and the futures of those that lived there. He told the Prince that he had no fear in going into that area because he knew that the Prince would be standing in the shadows close by, in case he would be needed.

As Will came into 'the village under the bridge,' he wondered how he would be received. Most who lived there were really undernourished and he was hoping that his fruit would be well received. But what most, if not all of those people didn't know, was the deep effects these fruits made on a man's mind, heart and soul and body. They didn't know how deeply a person's soul or character would be impacted.

So as Will began to enter the 'bridge village', he started quietly offering his unique fruit. He majored on the light pink fruit first because of its beauty and really likeable taste. He knew that he was an outsider, so he was trying to use ever skill he had to find a place not only in this 'village' but a place in their needy hearts. Without any fear he started going from one person to another. He knew that somewhere close by, somewhere in the shadows, was the power of the Prince. So Will moved as gently as he could with his loving fruit. Oh how he hoped that those there would eat the fruit and relish more and more of it.

Each time he would go back to his cart to get more fruit, he wondered if they would let him back into the area or would say to him, 'Go.'

As Will started back into the bridge village, as he called it, a large man stood in the middle of the path that Will was using. He confronted Will and said,

"You can't pass unless I get some stuff from you. This is my path and you have to pay to use it." Will quickly filled the man's hands with six different pieces of fruit. Then Will just stood there and encouraged the man by saying,

"Just eat some of it, Sir. If you like it I will get you more. I will give you as much as you want, so I can use your path."

With that the man began consuming the fruit like, well, like a wild man.

"I'll eat it all up and then you can get me more. And if you do that, I will let you pass," he said.

Many were watching the things that were going on between Will and giant George. That was his name. Even before George had eaten all of the fruit that Will had given him, a mellowing of his spirit started to come over him. A phenomenal gentleness came over him. The wild fire look that was in his eyes went out. The angry tension that was in his face seemingly dropped his chin. Although he was extremely tall, he had, for years, walked with a curve in his back. Suddenly he was standing up, not like an angry scary giant, but like a soft and gentle man over flowing with kindness and words of gentleness and meekness. The people who watched it happen became speechless when they saw what was happening. It made them want for themselves some of the fruit that Will was offering.

The third time Will went back to his cart, two of the men asked if they could help lighten his load and carry some of the fruit for him. Will was shocked and pleased at the same time. As he started back into the bridge village for the third time, many, if not all, started asking for seconds. Will was thrilled at the requests for seconds which he gladly fulfilled. As the evening progressed thirds and even fourths were freely offered.

Then different ones started coming up to Will and began to tell him that they had never in such a long time thought with so much clarity. They started telling Will of the storms of their souls that were settling down and for the first time in a long time, smiles were starting to show on their faces.

One said to him that for the first time in years he needed nothing. He felt so strong without any drugs. He wondered if he was going to be able to sleep because he was excited about how he was feeling.

Those who had initially refused the fruit began to see people they knew and knew well, changing right before their eyes. Those who had strongly said no to Will's help now were having a change of mind and were feasting on the fruit of the Garden of Life.

Will started using five or six men to carry armfuls of fruit into the village and loaded each one up with extras. Everybody was talking about new strength returning to their pain-filled bodies. The pains of the body were subsiding and health like they had not known for a long time, if ever, was taking place in them.

With the Young Prince quietly at Will's side, the walk back to the Garden that evening was one of the sweetest walks of Will's life. Will knew that the work had just begun, but what a beginning.

Half way home the preacher of the first church was out walking with miniature poodle and in a somewhat arrogant voice yelled at Will,

"Hey boy, throw me one of those fruits. I see your cart is full, so just toss me one."

Without a word of response, Will walked over to the pastor with one piece of fruit for his free hand and two more for his pocket. Then Will said to him,

"Enjoy. They are a gift. They're free," Will said, as he returned to his cart and continued on home.

While he sat on the front porch for a few minutes before he turned in, Will consumed two or three fruits with the red rings that the Prince called by the name LOVE.

13

PASTOR JOHNSON

As Will opened the gate to his garden the next morning, much to his surprise, there was Pastor Peter Johnson of the First Church, sitting against the wall of his Garden. It was clear that Pastor Johnson had not slept much the night before. Also, his face was in stress and tears.

Even before Will could get a word out of his mouth, the Pastor started talking a mile a minute through his sobs and tears. "Mister whatever your name is," he said, "I've been the leader of the crusade to clean up and get rid of the village underneath the bridge. I felt that it was a horrible eyesore and a cancer to our beautiful city's reputation. I didn't care where all those people were pushed to, they just had to go and go fast and yes, go far. But last night; yes, last night. Your fruit, yes, your fruit, made me so sick of myself that I have wept the night through. My tears have washed, it seems, my eyes clean of the blindness that was in them. I can't believe I was wanting to hurt and hurt deeply, so many people in so many ways, all in the name of God. Do you realize sir, I wanted to take a whole group of people and move them off of the face of the planet, all in the name of beautification.

"Mister, I need a lot of fruit. My attitude is plainly wrong. My eyes need to be cleaned up even more. Mister, I don't know what I'm going to do for those folks, but if God will touch me and give me ideas and His wisdom, I will do whatever I can to help them to be free at last from the bars on their minds, souls and spirits. I will do what I can even today to change their lot. I don't really know how to get them out of the condition they are in, but if God will show me what to do; I will do it to the best of my ability and with all of the resources of my church and family."

Will stood there stunned, speechless and, for a moment, very silent. Then he said,

"I think you can begin by, with the help of George the giant, as he is called, giving everyone in the village some of my abundant fruit for their help and healing. And for that matter, even you, right now, should have a couple of pieces to help you and to give you strength to climb the mountain you're going to climb to get done what you're talking about."

Then, as Pastor Johnson started to eat, a quietness descended on him. He just sat there next to the wall, eating a light green fruit called meekness. Then he moved on to a dark green fruit called gentleness. Finally one light peach fruit called love disappeared in a blink. With Will giving Pastor Johnson a 'hand-up,' the pastor stood there glowing as if a piece of sun was in his belly.

Just then an empty delivery cart was coming down the street. In no time Will hired the man to carry a cartful of fruit for Pastor Johnson down to the people in the bridge village. The results of this amount of fruit going to these people would end up transforming Pastor Johnson in ways he never thought would happen. In addition to changing Pastor Johnson, change started coming to the members of the First Church. It was said of the church that 'real people' started going there.

14

THE GARDEN OF CHAINS

As I got to know 'the gentle giant,' whose real name was George; I began to understand that north of our town was an area that was downright scary. Those that lived up there were poor and needy, as George put it, and some of them were beyond belief. Many people would not use the road in that area because they were sore afraid for their safety and money. He said,

"There was a weird old man up there that had a super large and quite over grown garden. He let anyone that wanted anything from it to just go in and get what they wanted. The problem was that your need for more of his fruit and food grew each time that you ate from that garden. Soon many addicted souls came from where ever they hid or lived, ate their fill and then seemingly crawled back into their huts or box houses to wait till the next day to come back to this plantation of misery."

He further told me that now that he knew what it meant to be free and at peace with the world, he could only conclude that up that way there were countless scores of people chained to the "garden of chains" or the "garden jail without bars," as he called it.

As I thought about this miserable place, I felt that that area deserved a visit from a Prince, a giant, and me, the gardener of the Garden of Life.

So, with a cart stacked high as I could, we three started heading north for this miserable area. As we got close to where this large weed infested garden was, we began to encounter people heading towards the Garden of Chains, as I called it, to get their fix of food. They all seemed to be driven to get to the garden to get something to eat. Clearly it didn't matter how many thorns or thistles, burrs or briars they had to go through to get food, getting food was all that mattered. The scratches and blood didn't matter. There was only one thing on their mind, fruit.

As we encountered folks I would have them sit down right where they were and eat my fruit. I was hoping that they would lose their desire to have whatever was in the Garden of Chains. Just as they would finish one piece I would give them another. Some would begin to stand up, having finished the first piece of my fruit and almost head for that garden but, hallelujah, they would sit back down and ask for more.

Soon these sad souls who had eaten in the garden that morning started leaving. What an awful mess. They were all scratched up from the previous days and also had today's cuts on them. Not only were they cut up, but they were, in some cases, violently sick. And even though full, they were starving and hungry.

Soon these sad, lost, miserable and defeated souls were sitting at the side of the road, eating one of my fruits and trying another. The more they sat there the more they attracted others who were coming down the road from the south and from the north to come to the fruit cart of Life, as I called it. Soon the area was filled with folks here and there and everywhere, eating to their fill.

As all of this was going on, the Young Prince quietly slipped across the road and just stood 'looking' at the Garden of Chains. It was such an overgrown jungle mess I thought that not even He could do much about it. Then, when it seemed that everyone was out of the Garden of Chains, he started walking down the road, looking intently at it. The more He looked and looked the more intense his stare became.

Then it started to happen. Vapors from the dissolving weeds and other plants began to fill the air. In no time, hovering over the Garden, was a yellow vapor cloud. And the more it grew, the more the garden dissolved.

As all of this was happening, scores and scores of people, young and old, men, women, and children, all addicts of this place sat filling themselves with my fruit. Suddenly, out of the blue they started to cheer as they saw the garden dissolving right before their eyes and their own personal transformation that was becoming visible for all to see. Soon almost a violent cheering was in the air as they watched, ate, and changed.

Then out of the Garden came an old wrinkled man, screaming,

"You're killing my garden. Stop it now. You're killing my garden. Stop it, stop it, and stop it now. I'm going to have nothing left. You're taking all of my life from me. You're going to end up killing me. Stop it and stop it now"

Even above the cheering throng you could hear his voice screaming at the top of his lungs.

At the sound of the old man's angry, hateful voice, the Prince turned away from looking at the Garden and looked at him. As their eyes met it seemed that the old man somehow recognized the Prince. As they looked at each other, it caused the old man to collapse in a heap in the middle of the road. All he looked like was a ball or heap of rags. Then the Prince turned back to his staring at the Garden. As the old man lay there, I made my way over to him and left the distribution of the fruit to George.

With a couple of fruits in my hand I knelt down next to the man and with a sharp knife started cutting small bits of fruit for the old man who seemed to be wasting away, to suck on. I would hold a piece of fruit to his mouth and squeeze the juice into his mouth, hoping he would swallow it and maybe it would have some effect on him. With piece after piece I did this with no visible effect, it seemed. But then when I stopped for a second to cut more I heard his voice quietly cry out to me the words,

"More. Please don't deny me, more. I want to live. Please feed me so I can live and be free from the torture and chains that are holding me. Please help me. Please feed me and I think I'll be free."

'More' turned into a bit and then one bit turned into two bits of fruit. Soon he, with my help, made it to the side of the road and started to eat more and more on his own.

The cloud of the dissolving garden became huge overhead. That would only be because the garden was so large. The Young Prince continued to look and stare, stare and look at this jungle of chains.

As the destruction of the garden reached to the back of the property, more and more cheering erupted from the crowd. Now, with more arrivals, the noise was almost deafening; but the result was so thrilling. The fruit from this terrible garden, yea from this terrible world of addiction, was coming to the end and its master was becoming something new right before every one's eyes.

Finally, and with much fanfare, the last of the Garden of Chains was totally dissolved. Acres and acres of dirt were all that was left. The briars, and burrs, and the weeds and thistles were gone with no evidence of them ever having been there.

Then from the weakened voice of the old man I heard, "Can I call my garden now, The Garden of Freedom?"

As the morning sun began to shoot its rays of light and warmth across the sky, the old man of the garden stood to his feet. His back was straight; his hands were full of strength and his walk was that of a young man. He found some clean clothes and put them on. As he begin to walk around outside, those who passed by didn't even know who they were waving to. The deep lines that were etched into his face had mellowed and a smile that he never had used was almost glued in place. A bucket of fruit that Will had left was being consumed. Then, as he finished each one he would go out to where his garden had been and plant the seeds from Will's fruit. To his amazement, they began to grow out of the ground right away. He, with a smile, called himself, Mr. Amazing!

15

COME ON HOME MOM

As Will left his front gate that afternoon, two woman, two blocks away, saw him and began waving at him. Their waving seemed to say, 'Wait for us." Then in several minutes the two ladies arrived at where Will was, waiting for them.

At first Will did not know either of them. In a few seconds both of them had caught their breath. The younger of the two spoke first. As she started to speak, Will gave her a light green piece of fruit and to the other he gave a light blue piece. Even before the younger lady could speak, she had taken a big bite out of the piece that Will had given her.

"Late yesterday afternoon my mother came to my back door." It was clear by the way she gestured that she was the daughter and the other lady was her mother. "To be honest with you sir, I thought I would never see my mother again. I really didn't want to see her again, to be frank with you. Several years ago a number of difficult things happened to her. The way that she dealt with them was with bad drugs. Soon she lost everything, as well as control over her life. She was a mess and I just didn't want to see her again. I was so embarrassed; I wanted her out of my life. I guess you would say, 'out of sight and out of mind'. That whole idea was working well until yesterday afternoon. From out of the blue, there stood my mother at my back door. Quite honestly I didn't recognize her. Everything about her appearance was, well, cleaned up. Her face looked at ease. She didn't look like she had the last time I saw her. She didn't want to come into my house but only asked to sit in a chair on my patio and tell me her story. She told me first of all that you could help me to understand the parts that seemed, well, untrue.

She had such a quiet spirit about her I found it difficult believing that this was really my mother. She told me that several days ago you came into the community under the bridge and started handing out, of all things, different fruits. She told me that she had been very reluctant to try it, but finally ate one piece. She said that the instant release of pain in her actually shocked her. Then she told me that all of the fears in her that acted like wild demons went, as she put it, QUIET. Their torture of her had ended. She felt like she had been given brand new eyes. Her whole complete world within and without changed. She said that she felt like a thousand pounds of chains had evaporated from off of her body. Come on, Mister, by the way, could I have another piece of whatever that is?"

Before Gail could get back on track with her question she devoured another piece of fruit and asked for a fourth. As her mother stood there in deep humility, she, too, tried a deep orange piece of fruit. Then, like the dawning of the sun in the morning, a brightness and joy began to fill her face. Her eyes started sparkling like stars on a clear night. A smile, a kind of permanent smile, came across her lips. Then to Gail's shock and amazement, she saw it, too. For a few moments she just stood there silent, amazed and speechless. She saw this miracle coming over her 'Ma', as she put it. In it all she never realized what was coming over her and was at work in her.

Turning to her mother she said,

"Ma, to be honest with you, I need help at home. With the house, kids, and now my graphic arts business that has really taken off like crazy, I'm falling apart. I really need you to live with me and Mitch. I can't handle it all. Please Ma, you don't need me....can I have one more piece of fruit, Mister? Oh, what was I saying? You don't need me half as much as Mitch and I need you. Oh forget it, its settled. You're coming to live with us and that takes care of that."

Just as Gail finished her 'speech,' her husband walked up. As he did so, Will gave him a couple of pieces of fruit to eat. When Gail saw Mitch, she started talking a mile-a-minute to him about how her Ma was coming to live with them and bail her out and rescue her. To this, Mitch just said,

"Ok. And by the way, could I have one more piece of fruit to eat? That was out of sight."

Without saying a word to Will, the three then started walking down the street. It was such an encouragement to Will to see the two ladies walking hand in hand, mother and daughter.

Half way down the street Mitch yelled,

"What about these big beautiful seeds?"

Will yelled back, "Plant'em and watch the results."

Little did Mitch know how fast these seeds would grow. As he walked out into his big backyard three days later, the vines from the seeds that he had planted were climbing the fence. It was clear that there was going to be much fruit with which to nourish the family.

16

A NEW HOME FOR THE HOMELESS

It was being reported in the newspaper and on television that the Hagerty Hotel, which had been out of business for six months due to the new motel on the highway, was discovered to be fully furnished like the last day it was in business. Mayor Bean was putting one hundred thousand dollars into a fund to get the hotel ready to be reopened for new residents. All of the Bridge Community was being invited to move into it free for four months. Others were pledging real help with food, clothing, training and jobs, to get these people back on their feet. As soon as the last of the Bridge Community was safely moved to the hotel and out of the cold, it was hoped that hundreds of volunteers would come on a Saturday to throw every bit of left-behind junk into waiting dumpsters and to cut down every unsightly vine and weed to restore the area to a beautiful sitting park area.

And as it turned out, five weeks later seven hundred volunteers turned out for the big make over. Within hours the trash was gone, the Bridge community was in its new digs and everything that was growing that had no real use was cut down. Huge flower gardens were put in that ended up dazzling the eyes of everyone. No one could believe, at the end of the day, that once there had been a bridge community there, with so many people in it. Now, all of them were seeing measurable changes come to their lives because of Will's fruit.

Will kept the lobby of the newly cleaned up hotel well stocked with fruit. And the changes that came about in the lives of the people there amazed everyone.

So many found jobs and moved into their own homes or apartments that only half of The Victory House ended up being used.

17

GROUND HOGS UNDER THE GARDEN

Usually the evenings were almost totally and completely silent. Yet, as Will sat on his front porch just quietly relaxing, he could hear, well, to describe it would be hard, but it was there. Sometimes stronger than at other moments, but It Was There.

As the young Prince sat down, Will could tell that he could hear it, too. Then turning to Will, he said something that caught him off guard.

"Will, I know you are constantly walking through your garden checking this and checking that, but have you ever walked around your garden wall outside? You know, Will, the outside is really connected to the inside. In short, I think you might want to get up and do a 'look see' of the wall outside. It could be quite enlightening. And because there is still a lot of light left, why not get going right now on your inspection tour of your stone wall."

Without a comment Will got up and left the garden at the front gate to do his little tour. No more had he gotten to the north side of the wall, than he discovered a fresh mound of dirt right next to the wall. Right next to the dirt was a hole going down; well it looked like it was going down, underneath the wall. As he looked down the wall, he saw a second mound of dirt and sure enough, another big deep hole. Quickly he returned to where the Prince was and shared what he had found.

"Well Will, the enemy has taken another form and is working in another place, but with the same goal-- to destroy your Garden of Life. The holes have been made by a family of ground hogs. It seems they never sleep but dig, dig, dig. They work to weaken a foundation by burrowing underneath it so that not even the foundation is sitting on anything. Then the weight of wall can't be supported and the wall will fall in. Let's go Will. If we don't get rid of them now, they will do irreparable damage to the wall."

In no time at all, the Prince had constructed a huge cage with a trap door in the middle of it.

"Will, when the ground hogs go into the cage and through the door in the middle of it, they won't be able to back up and get out because it's a kind of trap door. Once we get them all out and trapped in the cage, I will have someone take them way north of town and release them," said the Prince.

Soon there were wire cages sitting over each hole.

"Because 'hogs' don't like water," explained the Prince, "just start pouring water into each hole, one at a time, and we will see what will happen. It's going to take many buckets of water, so get a very large container and maybe we can get them to come out with the first bucket." Soon Will was ready, and with a nod from the Prince, released all the first buckets water at once into the first hole. Within a matter of seconds, flying out of the hole came three big adult ground hogs. And low and behold, the release of the second bucket of water into the second hole brought out three more. These were much younger, but nevertheless, they were ground hogs. Or you could say, 'trapped' ground hogs.

Although all of them had been caught, filling in the holes that they had dug was no easy task. They had already constructed quite a tunnel system underneath the foundation of the wall. Now, at night Will would once or twice a week walk around the wall on the outside. He now knew there were more enemies against him than he ever knew. He just had to be vigilant against the tools and plans of the enemy against His Garden of Life.

18

CONSTRUCTING MORE THAN A BUILDING

It was quite early in the morning. The sun had just popped its head above the horizon as Will was off, pushing his well filled fruit cart down the street toward an area known as 'city center.'

As he got into that area, he found that, much to his surprise, a great deal of construction was going on everywhere. One particular spot was a new massive shopping building that was under construction. As he was passing, it he could hear the boss of the construction crew. He had a voice that was the loudest you can imagine. His choice of words was the worst possible. There was no question about it, he was the boss.

Will noted where his outdoor desk was, and he could tell that his lunch cooler was right next to the desk.

As the boss walked away for a moment into the job sight, Will slipped over to his desk, opened his cooler, put in three fruits, closed it and put two light pink fruits on top of the cooler for the foreman to see, hopefully soon.

Then Will was about his business. As he went down the street just a little ways he saw five men pouring cement.

"Hey guys, when you get a chance, try out my fruit. I'll stack some up here for you to try when you take a break."

Without a drop of reaction the men continued on with their heavy task.

Every where he could, Will was stacking up his fruit for the construction men to try when they stopped for their morning break. In a kind of happy, joyful way, doing this just tickled Will. Men were going to start eating his fruit in a little while and not even know where it came from. As it turned out, Will had stacked up more than twenty piles of fruit all around the construction site. Oh was this going to impact the Center City Construction Crew.

Will was going to make sure that Giant George made a stop tomorrow with his horse drawn cart with another gift of fruit to this

C. C. C. C.

Even though Will had left a great deal of fruit around the job site, he still had a cart full to try to give away.

Then a solemn procession came down the street, a funeral procession. In deep respect for the funeral procession, everyone, including Will, left the street, and stood silently as it passed.

Will really felt compelled to do something. So as he stood there on the edge of the road, he started handing samples of fruit to all who went by. By the time the last person passed had received their fruit, the sounds of the funeral procession were almost gone. The crying that had characterized the procession was now almost gone. There was a deep quietness about the long line of mourners.

By the time they reached the cemetery, a peaceful calm prevailed over the throng of mourners. At the end of their time at the grave site they even broke into a song of joy and thanksgiving. People chose to hug and embrace each other like few had ever seen from a group of mourners.

Later, many would seek out Will for 'more' fruit, as they put it. Seeing a kind of joyous grave site of people ended up being talked about by many people. It was such an unheard of event that it was as you would say, 'the talk of the town.'

Will thought he would take a risk and stop by the county jail and give a load of fruit to the kitchen to put on the trays for the prisoners. Many of those that were in this jail had been convicted of their crimes and were locked up in this place for several years. Will had no way of knowing if the fruit would be accepted, and then distributed to the prisoners. And Will had no way of knowing if the prisoners would even try the fruit or what the effect on them would be.

But immediately at the beginning of the next day, a wagon from the jail was at Will's gate, waiting for him to open it. As he did so the guard who had driven the wagon gave Will a letter from the warden which said,

"Please sir, please. Can we have more fruit to give to the prisoners? Almost instantly there was an end to the hostility in most of the inmates. A calm came over the whole inmate population like I have never seen in my life. Please sir, help me with a gift of your fruit for my inmates." Signed, Warden Brown.

Will's reaction? In no time at all, he, the driver of the cart, and George filled the cart with many crates of fruit for the prison.

It was reported that men who had been angry, hateful, and violent were changed into good and gentle men. Their whole attitude changed to one of deep respect for the jailers and their situation.

Over the next weeks many started meeting with people they had hurt to seek their forgiveness. The words that were heard so much at the prison were repentance and forgiveness. Men were writing letters, begging for forgiveness. People found it hard to believe that this was going on and that it was genuine.

On Sunday a large room that had never been used for anything in the jail became their 'place of worship.' Church in this room became a packed church. It seemed that everyone came there on Sunday morning to calmly and quietly worship and pray.

Within the wire fence of the prison there was a lot of undeveloped land. Soon prisoners were planting all the seeds from the fruit they were eating. Of course in no time they were all shocked as they saw vines, bushes and young trees growing in just days. Almost immediately scores of prisoners were out in that area pulling every weed that stuck its ugly head up. That whole area became weed free and every plant well watered. Soon there was an abundance of fruit for everyone in the prison. Later in the year there was such a plentiful amount of fruit in this garden that 'free' box were set out on the street for people to take as they passed by.

So often, those that have been in prison return again and again after they have been released. They, it seems, go out and commit more and more crimes. For awhile it wasn't even being noticed but then one day the warden caught it. Men weren't coming back. They were staying out of prison because they were staying clear of crime. By year's end, one third of the prison cells were empty. With fewer prisoners to eat it, more fruit was placed at the side of the road. The more that was set there, the more it disappeared.

19

THE FARMERS MARKET

One day Gail and her mother came to Will's garden gate looking for him. As he opened his gate, there they stood with a bag full of, they didn't know.

They shared with Will that they had been to the farmer's market and there they saw some fruit being sold under the title "Will's Fruit." It didn't take much for Will to recognize the fruit of the Stranger. He knew it well and knew who was selling the fruit at the market.

The first thing he decided to do with Gail's help, her mother's, and John's, was to load up a large wagon with fruit and send them to the market and set up a booth of "Real Will's Fruit." He told them,

"Don't sell it. Give it away. I will get the Young Prince and see what he wants to do with the booth of bad fruit at the south end of the market."

And with that the two ladies and John were off. Will went running to the back of the garden to where the Prince was and showed him the Stranger's fruit, telling him all about where it had come from. He further told the Prince about the two ladies and George going to the Farmer's Market with his fruit.

For several seconds the Prince just stood there contemplating what to do. Then he flipped up his hood on his robe and said simply to Will,

"Let's go. Let's go fight for the souls of men, woman and children. "

Will could see a fire beginning to burn in the Young Prince's eye. He wanted to confront the Stranger or whoever was running the bad fruit booth. He not only wanted to confront them but he wanted to eliminate them. He wanted them to have no part of this so called fruit business.

As they started heading for the market, the stride of the Prince was large and fast. He really had a mission in his mind and on his heart. This was going to be tough. Nothing about it was going to be pretty. It was all Will could do to keep up with him. He had to start jogging to keep up with the pace of the Prince. Truly, they were going to war.

Even a long way off the Prince could see the counterfeit fruit booth. He could see that the Stranger had several men working for him. No matter where Will looked he could see person after person lying at the side of the road or out in the fields, violently sick. Will knew the feeling well and felt great compassion and empathy for them. These poor souls couldn't help themselves. All they could do was to lie in the dust and the fields and vomit. They were so sick they could hardly stand and could barely walk.

Then Will saw George in the distance and started waving his hands to get his attention. In no time George was standing in front of Will. Will explained that the only hope for these people was his fruit, or, that is, the fruit of the Prince. Will told him to run and get Gail and her mother and bring the cart with some fruit on it so all the people who were at the side of the road and in the fields could have some of his fruit to eat. Will knew their only hope was his fruit.

Like a shot George was off and in no time he and the two ladies were handing out 'good' fruit so the sick could eat and recover. Most wanted seconds and thirds after they had downed their first piece of the Garden of Life fruit.

There were a number of people around the Stranger's booth, which allowed the Prince to get really close to the Stranger before he was noticed.

Softly the Prince walked up directly behind the Stranger. Then in a flash he reached out and grabbed him and pulling him away from the booth He literally threw him through the air and out of the farmer's market. He flew so far that one thought for a moment that a turkey vulture bird was in the area. Where and how he landed no one knew and for that matter, and no one cared. Then the Prince over-turned the fruit table and ran the Stranger's helpers off.

As people began to eat from George's cart he became surrounded by a begging mob of people who wanted more and more of his healing fruit, which he was happy to distribute.

What a day it turned into. George and the two ladies were overflowing with joy and gladness. All they could talk about was everything they had seen.

All Will could talk about was, again, the defeat of the Stranger.

Little did Will know it but construction workers in the center city project were acting in quite an indescribable way. Their language, their courteous actions, their respectful actions towards their leaders and bosses were so profound that even those who were changed were talking about their own change. And the boss; well everyone thought he had been mentally electrocuted somehow. His words were, well, it's been described this way, 'Grace seasoned with love'.

Over the next week the job site became an example of spotlessness. Even though a lot of work was going on there, it was kept so spotless, that it started to be the talk of the town. Not only was this huge job site spotless, but the completion of the work accelerated. Soon it was believed that this huge project would be completed months ahead of time and way under budget. It was even being noted by everyone that the quality of the work that was being done was of the highest grade.

20

<u>THE MAYOR GETS A FRUITFUL SURPRISE</u>

The news was everywhere. In a week, the Mayor was celebrating being in office for twenty-five years. He had been in office that long because he had done a good job everyday he was Mayor. People were being encouraged to send a 'thank you' note to the Mayor, thanking him for his twenty-five years of service to the town.

As Will read that in the newspaper, he showed it to the Prince. After reading it, the Prince asked Will a somewhat startling question,

"What are you going to take and give to the Mayor?

For a moment Will was a little dumb founded and didn't come up with an answer.

"Well," said Will. "I don't think that I have anything that would fit the occasion. And by the way, who am I that I should give a gift directly to the Mayor?"

"Again," said the Prince, "What can you give to the Mayor?" Will quickly came back at the Prince and asked, "Well, do you have any ideas, Sir?"

For a moment the Prince just stood there, allowing Will's mind to do some thinking about his question. Then he said to Will,

"Why not take the Mayor a nice sampler basket of fruit. Load it up with three or four of all your fruits. I'm sure he will enjoy having that in his office so that he will have something to give to everyone that comes in to see him."

The idea hit Will right between the eyes. In no time at all he had picked four each of every kind of fruit he had in his Garden of Life. In no time at all he had gone down the street to the general store and found a big wonderful basket and some red ribbon to tie on to it.

The next morning Will was off for the city center area to give the Mayor a gift from his Garden of Life.

The basket looked splendid as he pushed his cart, with the basket sitting on it, down the street toward the office building of the Mayor. He was really happy that he had a small delivery cart to help him get the fruit into the Mayor's office. Thirty-six pieces of fruit is much heavier than one would think. But with the help of a couple of men that came along, Will and his big gift made it quite easily into the office building and to the Mayor's office.

As Will came into the lobby of the office building he was taken aback by what was in the center of a large table in the center of the lobby. It was a bowl of the Stranger's fruit! At that moment no one was in the lobby, so in an instant Will had filled a nearby trash can with the Stranger's fruit. He knew what it could do to anyone who tried it.

As he came into the office area of the Mayor, he was pleasantly surprised to have the Mayor standing there.

Those who assisted him were in a special meeting, which had left the Mayor all alone.

Quickly the Mayor introduced himself to Will and asked his name and all about him. After giving the Mayor his name and what he did, he picked up his basket of fruit and turned to gave it to him.

"I don't know if I really want it or not," said the Mayor. "That guy who was here yesterday, well he gave me some fruit too, but it really has made me sick down deep inside of me and low and behold, even though it has, I keep eating it." As the Mayor talked, he turned and pointed out another big basket of fruit. Will immediately recognized it as being a sampler of the Stranger's fruit.

Will had arrived just in time. The Mayor was becoming addicted to the fruit. He was already in deep trouble. Grabbing a waste paper basket, Will filled it with the Stranger's fruit. Then turning to the Mayor, he offered him some of his fruit.

"Sir," said Will, "I guarantee you will like this fruit much better and it will cure you almost instantly if you try it right now."

Although the Mayor was quite skeptical, he reached out and took the very light blue one. It tasted so good that he sat down behind his desk and just feasted on Will's gift. Even the Mayor's whole body began to growl and make noises as the fruit began to immediately heal his body.

The Mayor sat in his chair, amazed as to what was happening to him. As his staff arrived he ordered the building cleansed, as he put it, of all that horrible fruit and replaced throughout the building with Will's 'healing fruit.'

The Mayor's face that had been filled with tension and almost anger began to mellow as a tranquility that was almost unheard of descended upon him.

Truly Will's gift was a gift that kept on giving. In less than three hours, Will and George had returned with a small mountain of fruit that they placed throughout this governmental building.

It was quite a satisfying feeling knowing that one of the attacks by the Stranger had been thwarted. With a heart of great humility Will was so happy that he could honestly say, "The Stranger has lost again.

21

DOWN IN THE DUMPS

BUT NOT FOR LONG

Surprisingly, it seemed that as the days passed, Will was spending more and more time just sitting on the front porch of his home. His interest in doing or going was fading from his desires. His time napping even increased in the afternoon. Then early to bed and 'late' to rise. In a matter of days Will was doing nothing around the garden or around the city with his cart. I guess you could say, 'he just didn't care.'

It seemed that whatever he was constructing in his life, the Prince was going to let him deconstruct, at least it seemed that way for the moment.

By the end of the second week Will was in tough shape.

His motivation had sunk to zero. In his mind he had no interest in what he had done in the past. The thing that was becoming a little scary was the fact that Will wasn't even eating. No fruit and no water…nothing. He even got to the point that he wasn't even speaking to the Prince.

Finally, one evening the Prince sat down next to Will on the front porch. Looking at Will he just said one word,

"Enough."

The Prince was so forceful that it even made Will sit up and stare right at him.

The Prince looked him in the eye, now that he had gotten Will's attention, and began to ask him important questions.

Soon Will's comments and answers matched his attitude, confusing. His comments clearly were baseless and self serving. He thought the world was all about him. He felt, he said, so neglected. No one had taken time to get to know him or listen to him. He went on, and on, and yes, on about his poor condition. It seemed that his memory of the intervention of the Prince into his situation to set him free from the Stranger had almost if not, been forgotten. It seemed his memory of the victories he had experienced and seen were just a fading memory.

There Will sat, with a miracle garden staring him in the eyes. A high wall for beauty and protection. Food without end. The presence and power and plan of the Prince for his life. But for Will, it seemed that he could only see as far as half way down his nose. He couldn't even see the tip of his nose. With this outburst over, Will got up and went to bed and the sun was still up.

Early the next morning Will got up, washed up and walked out onto the front porch.

To him, life had become everything for others. Do for them. Give to them. Who was taking time to see to his interests, his wants and his desires, his hopes and his dreams. Oh, he enjoyed his digs, and fellowship with the Prince was unique, but he didn't have a deep friendship with anyone. He had no one investing any time in his life. Yes, he glad he was healthy but, but, but…

Will was all wound up and he couldn't find the button to set himself free from the tension, anxiety and his state of mind, which was NEGATIVE.

As he sat on the front porch, the Prince walked up to him with a loaf of bread. It was extremely warm, and it had real butter on it. Will could only say one thing as he ate it,

"How good, how good, AND how goooood."

"What in the world is the name of this bread, your Majesty?"   "Nearly three-thousand years ago it was called Angel's bread. Today it's called whatever you want to call it."

He said that the amazing thing is that the bread is the same today as it was those many years ago. The Prince further said that although the fruit of the Garden is unusual and does things that can't even be explained, this bread of the Angels does some special things also. There is a measureable change in a person who eats this bread. There seems to come to the person that eats this bread consistently a new sense of wisdom. He seems to know and understand things differently as he consistently eats this bread. Then when he adds the fruit of the Garden of Life, his change becomes apparent and after awhile this change becomes permanent.

In no time at all the loaf was gone, but the Prince made the promise of more bread later on today and certainly tomorrow. He explained to Will that he had a little bake shop about a block from here on a side street called Sheraton Alley. The Greenwood Bakery baked the bread for him according to his recipe

The Prince went on to suggest to Will that maybe George could go here and there with a cart of bread each morning and give it to whoever he will. That idea struck a positive note in Will.

Then to Will's surprise the front gate opened and low and behold, there was a line of people standing outside, waiting to come in and see him. I wonder who put the desire to do that in their hearts?

Even before Will could open his mouth, Charlie from across the street started in on Will. For ten minutes Charlie told Will about what he had come to mean to him. He told Will that there was a total change in his life and for that matter it had come into his parents' lives.

Then Gail and her mother shared with Will everything that had happened in their lives and now their home and in Gail's marriage and children. Gail's business was really doing well and she and Mitch, her husband, were finding more and more time to spend with the children, even though a lot of things were going on. Then there was their involvement with different people in the city that were in great need of what they called 'fruit care.' They said that even though they were busy, this was a fun and the most satisfying part of their lives, no doubt. But they made clear to Will that without him weeks ago and on a daily basis, their lives would fall apart.

George wanted to speak for hours and could have, but simply said,

"You're the man, Will. I am what I am because of your care and love for me. Oh, the fruit is great, but the fruit giver is so much more."

Pastor Johnson stepped in and said,

"Every part of my life has been totally transformed. Imagine Will, if you hadn't given me just one little piece of fruit, just imagine what I would be, my church, would be, my home would be, and yes what our city would be. You, the giver of fruit, changed me from top to bottom, hallelujah and AMEN!

Those who had mourned told about their change within. They talked about death being filled with comfort and joy.

Construction workers rejoiced at their new desire to do good work without being told to.

The angriest man in town just walked up to Will's porch and fell down and openly wept. "Hallelujah," he cried, "old things have passed away. I am a brand new man."

The line was long and went on for some time with people telling Will of his value and importance in their lives. They loved the fruit, but told Will that to give fruit you first have to have a 'heart of fruit,' a 'mind of fruit,' and a soul that is full of fruit.

As they finished, the rag that Will had in his hand was soaked with his tears. Then without saying a word, Will got up, walked over to his fruit cart and pushed it out of the gate, heading for today's adventure in fruit giving.

It's been several years now, but each and every morning you can see Will pushing his fruit cart to another fruitful adventure, as he put it. Now go thou and do the same.

WORDS FROM BROTHER DAVID

There is a real stranger who wants to destroy your values, your joy and, if he can, your life. If you let him, his seeds of destruction will grow, and his fruit will control you and finally destroy you, as it has done to millions of people down through the years.

There is also a real Prince knocking at the door of your life. He can put some miraculous things into your life that will be there for all time and all eternity.

Open up your life to the Prince, the Lord Jesus, who died for you. He is the only one who can plant love, joy and peace within you. His seeds will cause love and forgiveness, and hundreds of other qualities to bloom in you for all of time. Is it any wonder that they call Him the Prince of Peace, the love of God?

Behold, I stand at the door and knock.

If any man hears my voice and opens the door

I will come into him and fellowship with him

And he with Me. Revelation 3:2

Blessings on you,

D

Brother David

If you want more information, please contact me at:

brotherdavid1216@gmail.com

For more titles by Brother David visit: **AMAZON.COM**

FOR KIDS:

Freddie the Frog

Alsie's Bible

Big Jim

The Great Wall of the Jungle

Christmas Eve at Your House

The Adventures of the Pink Kite

The Chevrolet that wanted to be a Cadillac

Peter and the Clay

Tales from the Pond—

(contains both Freddie The Frog and Cecil the Dragonfly)

FOR JUNIORS:

The Black Chalice (Book I)

The Revenge of the Black Chalice (Book II)

Delivery of the King (Book III)

The Mountains of Great Deception (Book IV)

Made in the USA
Columbia, SC
09 June 2022